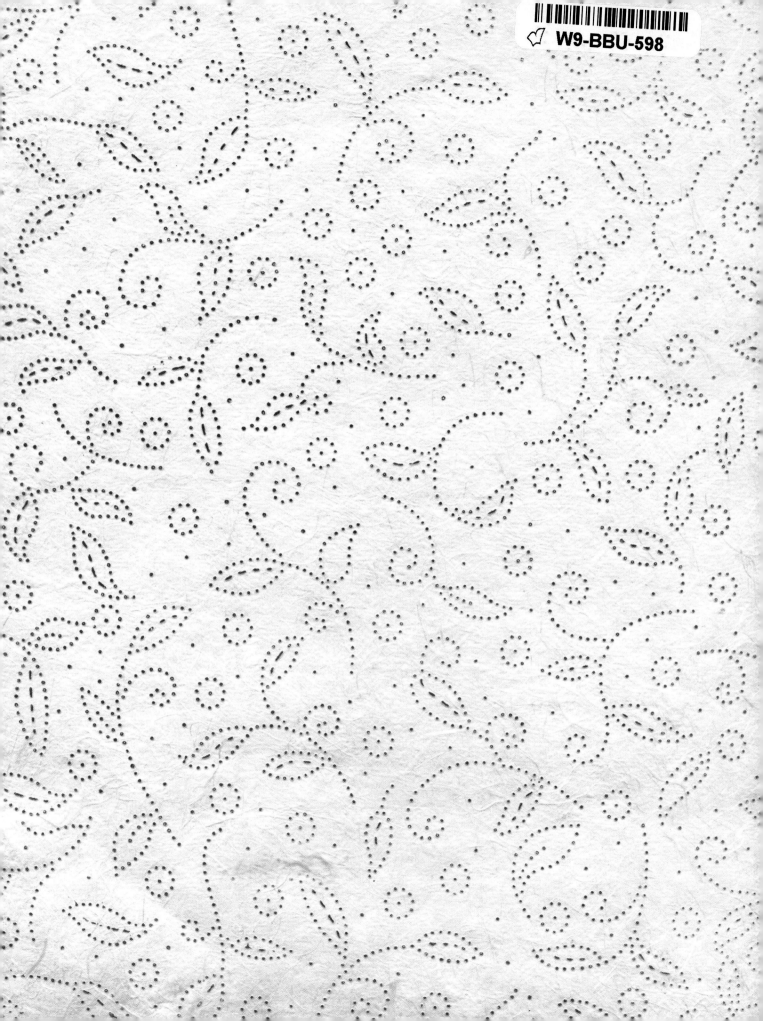

For Miriam and Shakirah. Thanks for the memories. *N.R.*

For Matteo Pittore, who gave me the courage
to set out on my creative journey. *V.C.*

JANETTA OTTER-BARRY BOOKS

Going to Mecca copyright © Frances Lincoln Limited 2012
Text copyright © Na'ima B Robert 2012
Illustrations copyright © Valentina Cavallini 2012

First published in Great Britain and in the USA in 2012 by
Frances Lincoln Children's Books, 4 Torriano Mews,
Torriano Avenue, London NW5 2RZ
www.franceslincoln.com

A catalogue record for this book is available from the British Library.

ISBN 978-1-84780-153-1

Illustrated with collage and mixed media.

Set in ITC Usherwood

Printed in Shenzhen, Guangdong, China by C&C Offset Printing in October 2011

1 3 5 7 9 8 6 4 2

Going to Mecca

Na'ima B. Robert

Illustrated by Valentina Cavallini

F

FRANCES LINCOLN
CHILDREN'S BOOKS

Come with the pilgrims
As they set out on a journey,
A journey of patience
To the city of Mecca.
Some call the Hajj 'the journey of a lifetime'.
Fly with the pilgrims
As they make their way there.

Dress with a pilgrim
As he stands barefoot,
A sheet round his shoulders,
Another round his waist.
Now he is the same as thousands of others,
No riches or status
To tell them apart.

Call with a pilgrim
As she utters a prayer,
And says the words
That will make her draw near:
"*Labbayk Allahumma labbayk.*"
"Here I am, O my Lord, here I am."
And above and around her
Thousands of others
Are making the call
Exactly like her.

Gaze with the pilgrims
As they look at the Black Stone,
The Black Stone that was sent
down from the Heavens.
Those nearby kiss it,
Those far away point to it,
Just as their Prophet did, so long ago.

Stand with the pilgrims
As they face the Ka'bah,
Head bare, feet in sandals,
With thousands of others,
Strangers, sisters,
Strangers, brothers.
They stand and then move
Like a great swirling sea.
Round and round
The great crowd surges,
Like a whirlpool, a tornado
Of blurred faces and voices.

Pray with a pilgrim
As he stands, then bows,
And offers a prayer
At the station of Ibrahim.
Drink with a pilgrim
As he savours the sweetness
Of the blessed spring water
At the well of Zamzam.

Reflect with the pilgrims
As they stand on As-Safaa,
Thinking of Hajar,
The wife of Ibrahim,
Who searched the whole desert,
Finding no one to help her
As her son, Ismaeel, cried out with thirst.

Walk with the pilgrims
As they cross, just like Hajar,
The valley that lies
In between those two hills.
Where she ran and ran,
Backwards and forwards,
Seven times over,
Looking for water.

Weep with the pilgrims
As they think of her pain.

Wait with the pilgrims
As the ninth day approaches,
And the city swells
With pilgrims from all lands.
From city
And steppe,
From island
And desert,
They all congregate
To continue the journey.

Travel with the pilgrims
To the place they call Mina,
Where the great crowd will slumber
Until morning comes.

Go with the pilgrims
To Mount Arafat,
Where the great tide of people
Settles for the day.
And voices are raised
And hearts are emptied
As tears and cries pierce the desert air.

Now to Muzdalifah and then back to Mina,
Where they search for seven pebbles
To stone the Jamarat.
By now the crowd is surging,
They fight to keep their grip
As all around are bodies,
Dust, air and sky.

After the sacrifice
That will feed the poor,
The pilgrims shave their hair,
Make *tawaaf* and *sa'i* once more.
For they have crossed the stormy sea,
They have made it to the shore.
And now their bodies ache
And every limb is sore.

But, even so, their hearts race,
And their souls soar high and free,
For they have made that journey:
Feet in sandals, heads bare,
With thousands of others,
Strangers, sisters,
Strangers, brothers.

And now all the pilgrims
Are home from their journey,
Their journey of patience
To the city of Mecca.
The trip of a lifetime,
A pillar of faith.
Welcome the pilgrims,
Now home from the Hajj.

WELCOME HOME!

TAXI

About the Hajj

Hajj, the pilgrimage to Mecca, is one of the pillars of the Islamic faith – one of the five foundations of Muslim life. Every Muslim is required to perform Hajj at least once if he or she is able. A sincere Hajj is rewarded by the forgiveness of all your sins. Many of the rituals of the Hajj are related to the stories of the Prophet Ibrahim (Abraham) and his family.

The Black Stone
The Black Stone is set in a silver frame and fastened to the side of the Ka'bah. The Prophet Muhammad said that when the stone was sent down from Paradise, it was as white as milk but the sins of human beings turned it black.

The Jamarat
The Jamarat are three walls, originally three pillars. The stoning of the Jamarat with seven stones is another ritual that was inspired by Prophet Ibrahim who, when Satan appeared before him at the three Jamarat, threw seven stones at him. The pilgrims' stoning of the Jamarat symbolises this event.

The Ka'bah
The Ka'bah was built by the prophet Ibrahim and his son Ismaeel as a house of worship.

Sa'i
This is the rite of walking seven times across the valley between the two hills, As-Safaa and Marwah, retracing the footsteps of Hajar, the wife of Ibrahim.

The Station of Ibrahim
This is a stone that Prophet Ibrahim stood on while building the Ka'bah. If you look into the glass structure around it, you will be able to see two footprints embedded in the rock.

Tawaaf
This is the action of walking round the Ka'bah seven times in an anti-clockwise direction, while reciting prayers.

The Well of Zamzam
This well began as a spring that appeared when an angel struck the ground in answer to Hajar's search for water for her son, Ismaeel. The water is drunk for its blessings and curative properties.